# Home by Five

# Home by Five

*Ruth Wallace-Brodeur · illustrated by Mark Graham*

MARGARET K. McELDERRY BOOKS
NEW YORK

Maxwell Macmillan Canada · Toronto
Maxwell Macmillan International · New York · Oxford · Singapore · Sydney

Margaret K. McElderry Books, Macmillan Publishing Company, 866 Third Avenue,
New York, NY 10022
Maxwell Macmillan Canada, Inc., 1200 Eglinton Avenue East, Suite 200,
Don Mills, Ontario M3C 3N1
Macmillan Publishing Company is part of the
Maxwell Communication Group of Companies.

Printed in Hong Kong by South China Printing Co. (1988) Ltd.
First Edition    10  9  8  7  6  5  4  3  2  1

Library of Congress Cataloging-in-Publication Data
Wallace-Brodeur, Ruth. Home by five / Ruth Wallace-Brodeur ; illustrated by Mark Graham.
— 1st ed.    p.    cm.
Summary: Although Rosie knows that she has to be home by five
o'clock, there are many fascinating sights to delay her on the way.
ISBN 0-689-50509-4
[1. Tardiness—Fiction.  2. City and town life—Fiction.]    I. Graham, Mark, ill.
II. Title.    PZ7.W15883Ho  1992    [E]—dc20  90-39854

*For my mother,*
DOROTHY H. WALLACE

—R.W-B.


*To* ELLEN

—M.G.

"Home by five." Papa wound Rosie's scarf three times around her neck. "No excuses this time, Rosie. Be home by five at the latest."

"Maybe I should have a watch." Rosie's voice was fuzzy through the striped wool. "A blue one with colored numbers. Then I could tell when to hurry."

"The rink closes at four-thirty," Papa said. "If you come straight home, you don't need to hurry. It's only four blocks."

The music stopped at four-thirty. "Clear the ice," a voice boomed over the loudspeaker. "The rink is now closed until seven."

"Once more around," yelled Rosie's friend Josh. "Last one's a rotten egg."

"That's you, then." Rosie skated toward the gate. "I have to be home by five."

Rosie's skate lace was stuck in a knot.

Her boots were jumbled under the bench.

Her scarf got caught in her zipper.

"Can't catch me," Josh teased as he ran off with her hat. Rosie got it back, but she didn't take his. She had to be home by five.

Outside, falling snow danced tiny, cold tickles at Rosie's face. She tipped her head back and opened her eyes as wide as she could. She wanted to know how snowflakes would feel on her eyeballs, but her lashes flick-flicked them away before they could land. Rosie didn't have time to wait for her eyes to hold still. She had to be home by five.

The stone eagle above the post office door was wearing a pointed snow hat. "You look good in a hat," Rosie called politely. "Do you think the basement steps are ready for sliding?" She made a path around the side of the building and looked down the steep steps. They were rounded smooth as a marshmallow. No sliding today, though. Rosie had to be home by five.

Mrs. Peterson was getting ready to close the bakery. She had already taken in her big flag with the picture of a pie on it.

"Hello, Mrs. Peterson." Rosie knocked on the big glass window. Mrs. Peterson looked up from counting money at the cash register. She smiled and pointed to the frosted cream doughnut left between the rows of coconut and cinnamon spice. Frosted cream doughnuts were Rosie's favorites. Rosie waved sadly. She had to be home by five.

Rosie kept thinking about that frosted cream doughnut as she walked along. It would have taken only a minute, maybe less, to get it. But now she would have to walk all the way back....

Rosie stopped in front of Elmdale Apartments to think it over. A tiger cat was sitting in a first-floor window. He was bigger than Rosie's cat, Tam, but he stared at her in the same way, as though he knew exactly what she was thinking.

"Don't worry," Rosie said. "I'm not going back for the doughnut." She went close to the window to see if the cat had double paws like Tam's. He didn't, but he had a notch in his ear. Tam had one, too.

"How did you get that notch, cat?" Rosie asked through the window. The cat blinked, then yawned and looked away.

*"Notched ears,*
*Bloody noses,*
*Skinned knees…"*

Rosie swung around and around a sign pole, thinking of what came next. She had a rhyme all figured out by the time she reached the corner of her street.

*"Notched ears,*
*Bloody noses,*
*Skinned knees,*
*Stubbed toes-es.*
*Tough old cat,*
*Tough old me.*
*I cry.*
*Does he?"*

Rosie brushed the snow
from the window ledge of
Mattioli's Grocery. It was a
good rhyme. She would tell it
to Tam.

Lights shone up the sidewalk gratings from the dance studio in Mattioli's basement. Rosie could hear the piano pounding and the teacher counting: one, two, one, two. Sometimes Rosie lay flat on the grating so she could see all the way across the room to the mirror wall. Each dancer had a twin partner in the mirror. Today Rosie just bent over far enough to see the teacher's arms and legs stretch and fold to match the music.

"One, two, one, two," Rosie sang as she danced across the street in front of Mrs. Damon's house. Mrs. Damon's newspaper was lying on the walk at the foot of her steps. Rosie put it on the porch so it wouldn't get snowed on.

Then she ran the rest of the way. She would surprise Papa. She had come straight home. She had hurried the whole way. She must be home *before* five.

Papa met Rosie in the hall. So did Mama.
They didn't look very happy. They would
feel better when they saw how
early she was.

"Surprise!" Rosie shouted. "I'm home
before five!"

Papa was still frowning.

Mama's hands were on her hips.

"I didn't chase Josh and I didn't slide on the post office steps." Rosie was panting, she had run so fast. "I didn't watch the dancers and I even didn't get a frosted cream doughnut. There was only one left, but I had to be home by five."

Mama looked at Papa.

Papa looked at Mama.

They both looked at the clock behind Rosie.

"Oh," said Mama.

"Well," said Papa.

Rosie could tell they felt better already.

The next evening, Mama and Papa surprised Rosie. They gave her a watch. It had a blue band and colored numbers. They had frosted cream doughnuts for dessert.